JUSTIN ORDINARY SQUIRREL

written by Shawn A. McMullen
illustrated by Amanda Haley

CIP DATA AVAILABLE
Library of Congress Catalog Card Number 90-26946
Copyright © 1991, The STANDARD PUBLISHING Company, Cincinnati, Ohio.
A division of STANDEX INTERNATIONAL Corporation.
Printed in U.S.A.   24-03897

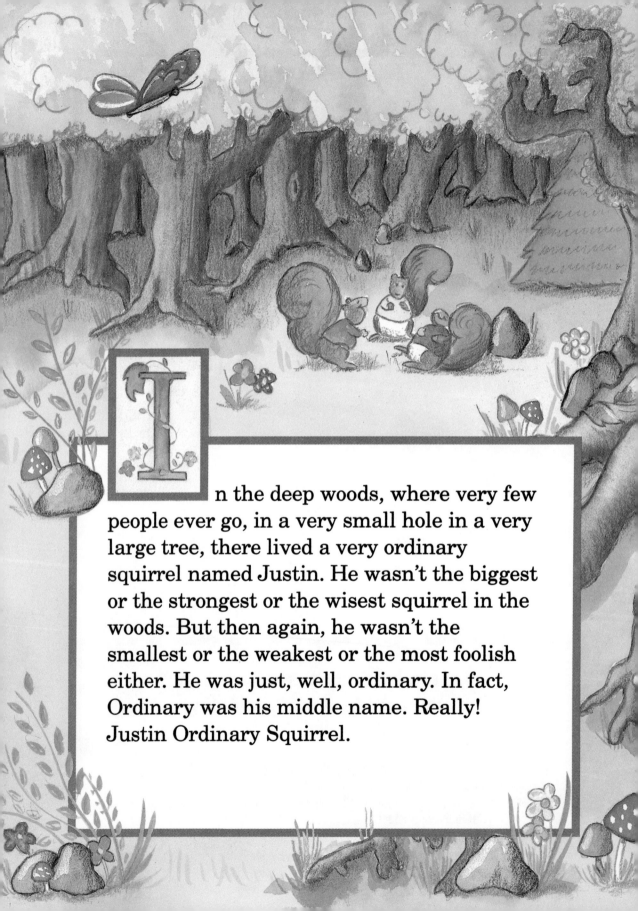

In the deep woods, where very few people ever go, in a very small hole in a very large tree, there lived a very ordinary squirrel named Justin. He wasn't the biggest or the strongest or the wisest squirrel in the woods. But then again, he wasn't the smallest or the weakest or the most foolish either. He was just, well, ordinary. In fact, Ordinary was his middle name. Really! Justin Ordinary Squirrel.

Now Justin didn't mind being ordinary. In fact, he rather liked it. He spent most of his days in the same ordinary way, playing with friends or munching acorns or napping in his hole in the tree.

"Being ordinary is just fine with me," he often said to himself. "This way you never have to worry about being the best, and you never have to worry about being the worst." Justin liked not having to worry about things. And so he never worried—well, almost never.

One chilly autumn evening found Justin and his friends enjoying a game of tree tag. As Justin was sneaking up behind another squirrel, ready to grab his tail, he heard the rustling of leaves below him.

He looked down in time to see the familiar face of a chubby little squirrel named Isaac as he ran through the woods just as fast as his little legs could carry him.

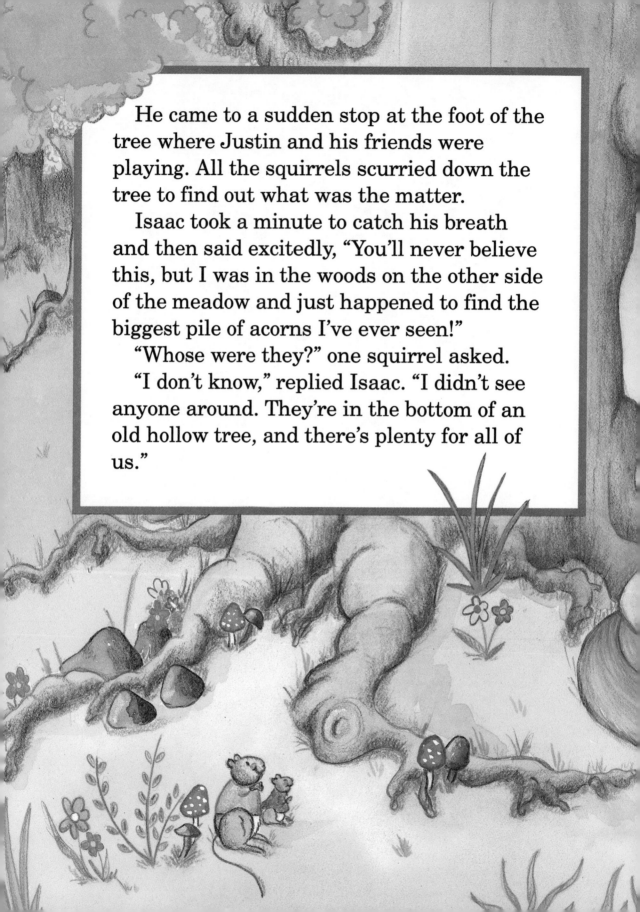

He came to a sudden stop at the foot of the tree where Justin and his friends were playing. All the squirrels scurried down the tree to find out what was the matter.

Isaac took a minute to catch his breath and then said excitedly, "You'll never believe this, but I was in the woods on the other side of the meadow and just happened to find the biggest pile of acorns I've ever seen!"

"Whose were they?" one squirrel asked.

"I don't know," replied Isaac. "I didn't see anyone around. They're in the bottom of an old hollow tree, and there's plenty for all of us."

"Wow!" said the squirrel next to Justin. "Think of all the work it would save us if they were ours. No more hunting and burying food for the long winter. We'd have all we need!"

"My thoughts exactly," added Isaac. "All we have to do is carry them off to our own hiding places."

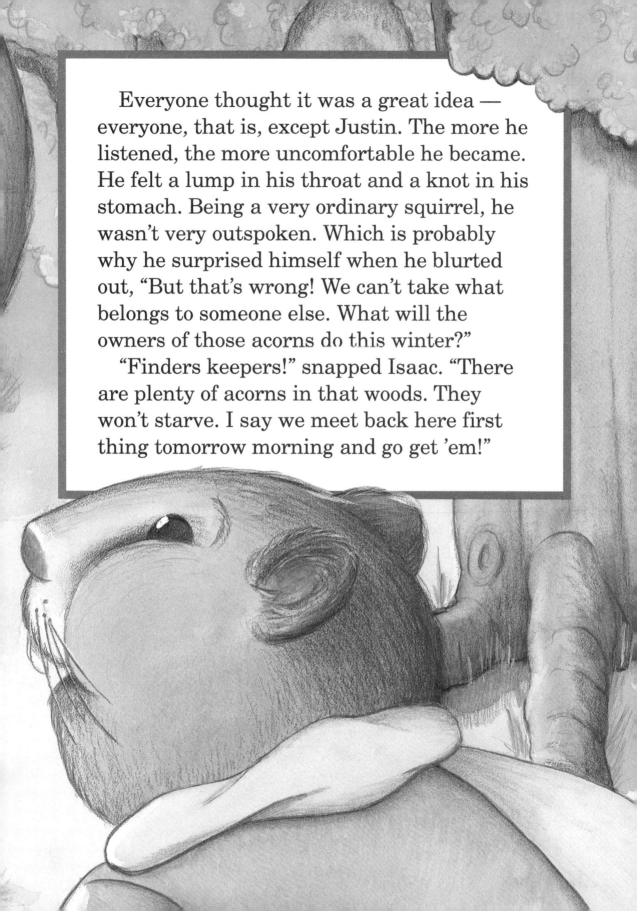

Everyone thought it was a great idea — everyone, that is, except Justin. The more he listened, the more uncomfortable he became. He felt a lump in his throat and a knot in his stomach. Being a very ordinary squirrel, he wasn't very outspoken. Which is probably why he surprised himself when he blurted out, "But that's wrong! We can't take what belongs to someone else. What will the owners of those acorns do this winter?"

"Finders keepers!" snapped Isaac. "There are plenty of acorns in that woods. They won't starve. I say we meet back here first thing tomorrow morning and go get 'em!"

Everyone agreed—everyone, that is, except Justin. While his friends continued to make plans, Justin slowly made his way back to his hole in the tree. He felt sad and lonely.

Night came, but Justin couldn't sleep. He could only think. He thought about his parents and all they had taught him as a young squirrel. And if there was one thing Justin had learned from them, it was that even the most ordinary squirrel must always try to do the right thing. Justin kept thinking. And somewhere, in the middle of all his thinking, he got a grand idea.

No sooner had he got it than he sat straight up in his bed and said to himself, "I'll do it!"

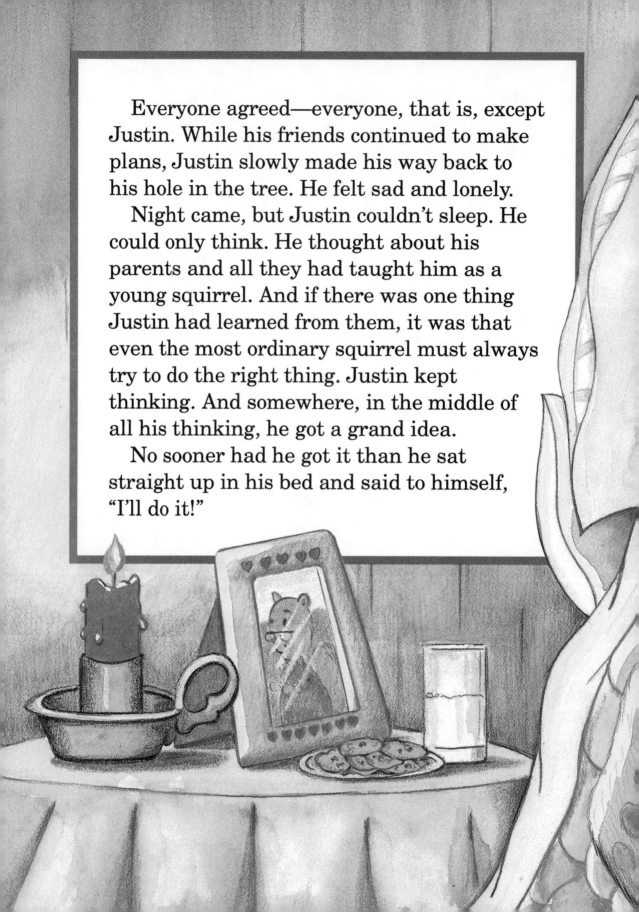

And with that he scampered out into the night and through the trees and across the meadow. He didn't stop until he came to the woods where Isaac had discovered the acorns.

He searched every hollow tree he could find. And that isn't a very easy thing to do in the dark. Finally he found the acorns.

"Does anybody live here?" Justin called up the tree.

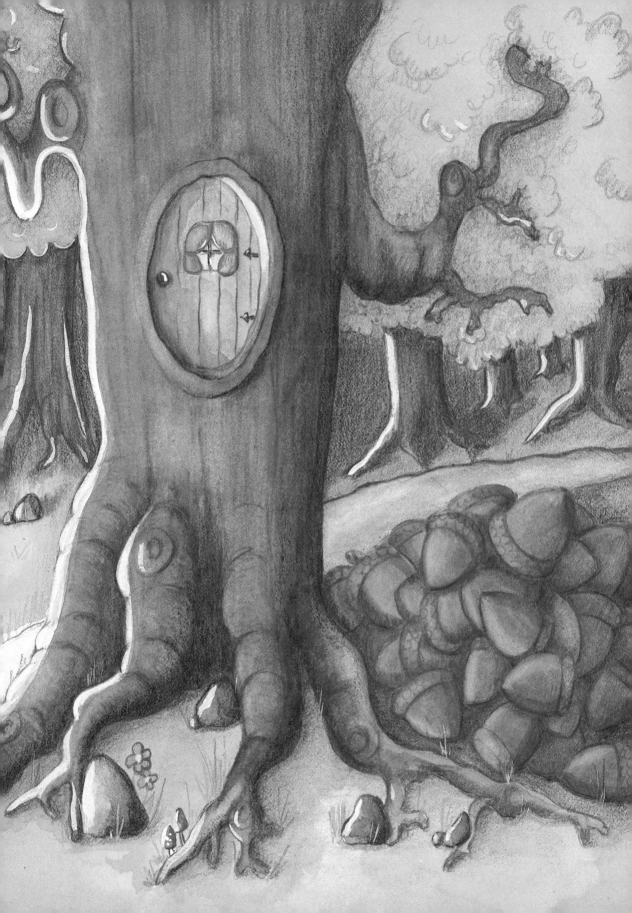

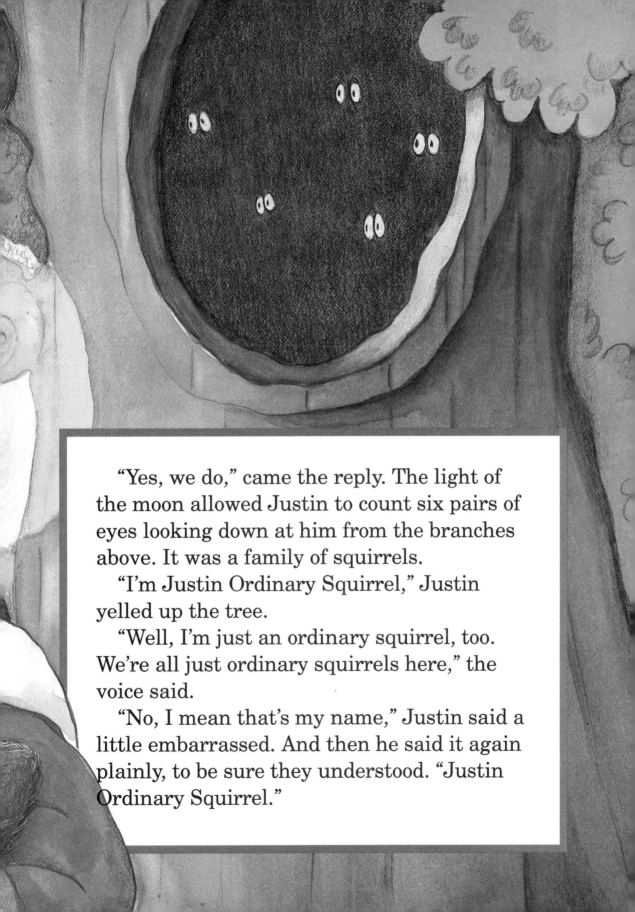

"Yes, we do," came the reply. The light of the moon allowed Justin to count six pairs of eyes looking down at him from the branches above. It was a family of squirrels.

"I'm Justin Ordinary Squirrel," Justin yelled up the tree.

"Well, I'm just an ordinary squirrel, too. We're all just ordinary squirrels here," the voice said.

"No, I mean that's my name," Justin said a little embarrassed. And then he said it again plainly, to be sure they understood. "Justin Ordinary Squirrel."

"Oh, I see," said the voice. "Well, what do you want at this late hour?"

"I came to tell you to move your acorns," said Justin.

"What for?" asked the voice.

"There are some squirrels who are planning to steal them," Justin replied.

"Who would do such a thing?" the voice questioned.

"I'd rather not say," returned Justin. "I'd just like to help you protect your belongings and keep those squirrels from making a big mistake."

"Then we've no time to lose!" shouted the voice.

Justin now saw that the voice belonged to the father squirrel. He led his family down the tree and they went to work at once. Justin helped too.

On through the night they carried the acorns from the bottom of the hollow tree to a special place the father squirrel knew about.

As they finished their work, Justin noticed that the sun was coming up. He breathed a sigh of relief. The exhausted squirrel family went back to bed in their tree without a word—not even a thank-you to Justin. But even so, Justin returned to his own tree and his own bed feeling quite satisfied.

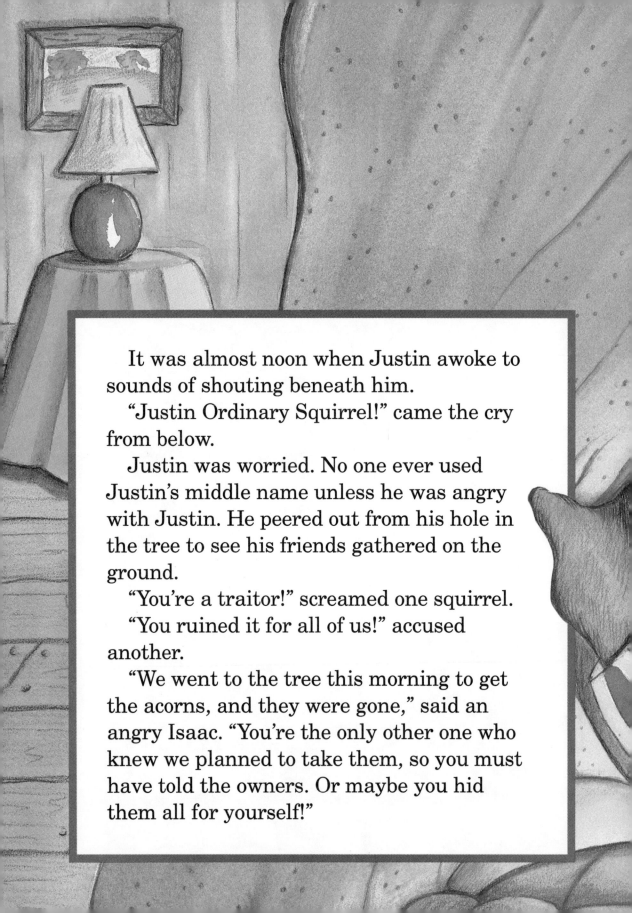

It was almost noon when Justin awoke to sounds of shouting beneath him.

"Justin Ordinary Squirrel!" came the cry from below.

Justin was worried. No one ever used Justin's middle name unless he was angry with Justin. He peered out from his hole in the tree to see his friends gathered on the ground.

"You're a traitor!" screamed one squirrel.

"You ruined it for all of us!" accused another.

"We went to the tree this morning to get the acorns, and they were gone," said an angry Isaac. "You're the only other one who knew we planned to take them, so you must have told the owners. Or maybe you hid them all for yourself!"

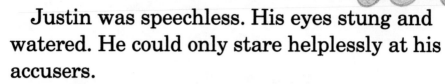

Justin was speechless. His eyes stung and watered. He could only stare helplessly at his accusers.

"Whatever you did, you're no friend of ours," concluded Isaac. The others agreed loudly. And then they left. In a moment the woods were quiet again.

Justin started to cry. "Oh, why did I even bother? I was only trying to do the right thing. Now everyone hates me!"

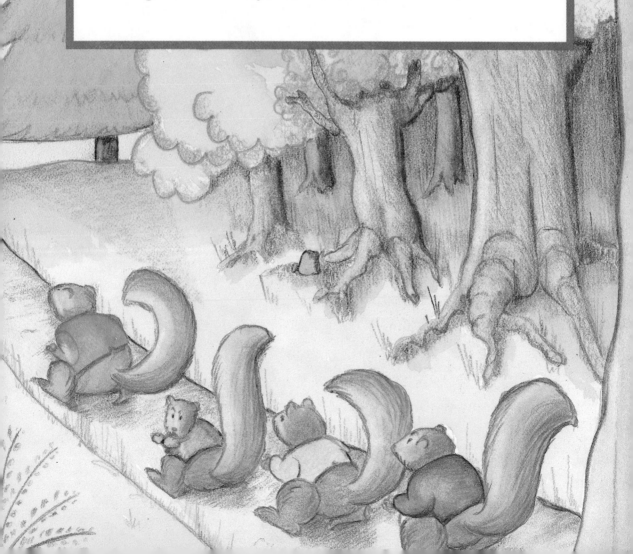

He was so upset he didn't notice the dark shadow until it had completely covered him. He looked up to see a thick, feathery body with large wings as it settled on the branch just above him. It was a great horned owl.

Justin turned to run because big owls like that are seldom friendly to little squirrels. But the voice of the great bird was soothing. As soon as Justin heard it, his fears vanished.

"I won't harm you, little one," the owl said, looking at Justin with brilliant yellow eyes. "I was roosting in that tall pine tree, and I saw how your friends treated you a moment ago." He lifted a wing slightly to show Justin where he had been. "Would you like to talk about it?"

And with that Justin told the owl the whole story. When he finished, the owl smiled an understanding smile. "You should be proud of yourself. What you did was no ordinary thing."

"I don't feel proud," Justin complained. "I feel sad and alone. I used to be just ordinary. Now I'm not even that. Everyone hates me!"

"Oh, I doubt that," said the wise bird. "I'm sure you still have many friends. But even if you don't, you can learn something very important from all this."

"And what's that?" asked Justin doubtfully.

"That when you have to make a choice, it's always better to do what is right than to try to please everyone around you," replied the owl. "That's exactly what you did last night. And you should be proud of yourself."

With that, the owl swooped out of the tree and disappeared into the woods.

Justin sat in his tree and thought about what the owl had said. And the more he thought about it, the more he agreed. It was important to do the right thing, just as he had been taught, even if he had to do it all by himself. "And even if no one else understands," Justin thought out loud.

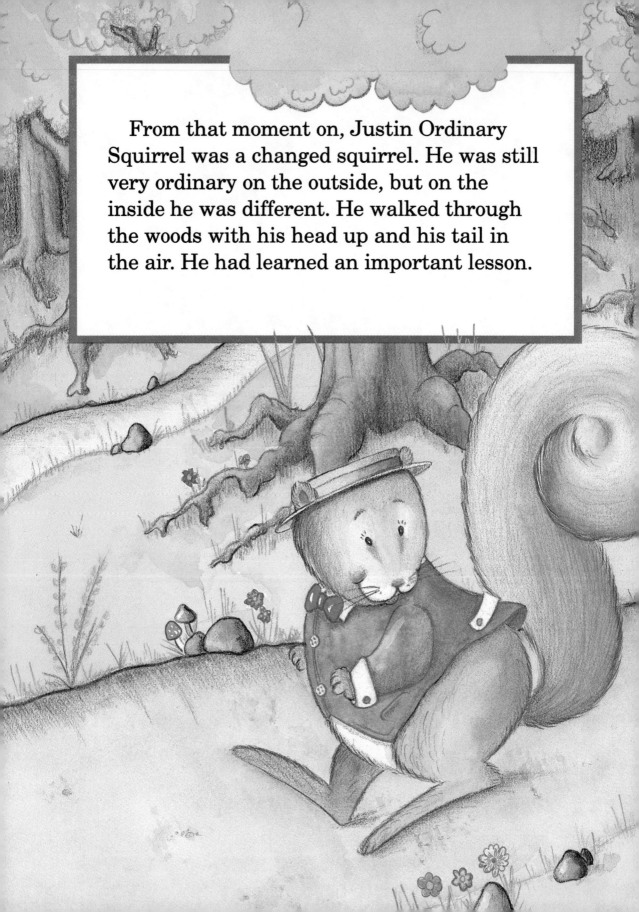

From that moment on, Justin Ordinary
Squirrel was a changed squirrel. He was still
very ordinary on the outside, but on the
inside he was different. He walked through
the woods with his head up and his tail in
the air. He had learned an important lesson.

And just as the owl had predicted, Justin's friends came back—at least those who were true friends did. Some of them even apologized for the way they had treated him. And whenever that happened, Justin Ordinary Squirrel looked them squarely in the eye, smiled his biggest forgiving smile, and said with all his heart, "Apology accepted."

"We must obey God, not men!" (Acts 5:29, ICB).